Dear Parent:

　　We're happy to share this latest book about Mrs. Toggle and her class with you and your child.

　　There's no better way to build strong bridges to your child's future success than to read with your child.　Here are some helpful reading hints for you and your child:

1) *Make a special family reading time — same time each day.*　Get into the habit of reading regularly.

2) *Trade books with other family members and friends.* Every family has favorite books — this is one good way to find some new favorites!

3) *Bring books along on trips, even short errands.*　A good book is always a good companion.

　　We hope you enjoy *Mrs. Toggle and the Dinosaur!*

Sincerely,

Stephen Fraser

Stephen Fraser
Senior Editor
Weekly Reader Book Club

MRS. TOGGLE AND THE DINOSAUR

Weekly Reader Book Club Presents

Robin Pulver

MRS. TOGGLE AND THE DINOSAUR

Illustrated by R. W. Alley

Four Winds Press   New York

Collier Macmillan Canada   Toronto

Maxwell Macmillan International Publishing Group
New York   Oxford   Singapore   Sydney

This book is a presentation of Newfield Publications, Inc.
Newfield Publications offers book clubs for children
from preschool through high school. For further
information write to: **Newfield Publications, Inc.**,
4343 Equity Drive, Columbus, Ohio 43228.

Published by arrangement with Four Winds Press, an imprint of
Macmillan Publishing Company. Newfield Publications
is a federally registered trademark of Newfield Publications, Inc.
Weekly Reader is a federally registered trademark
of Weekly Reader Corporation.
Printed in the United States of America.

For David,
who likes dinosaurs
—R.P.

For Cassandra
and Zoë
—R.W.A.

First American Edition 10 9 8 7 6 5 4 3 2 1
The text of this book is set in 16 point Berkeley Old Style Book. The illustrations are rendered in watercolor.

Library of Congress Cataloging-in-Publication Data ● Pulver, Robin. Mrs. Toggle and the dinosaur / Robin Pulver;
illustrated by R. W. Alley. - 1st American ed. p. cm. Summary: Mrs. Toggle and her class prepare for the arrival of a
new student whom they expect to be a dinosaur.
[1. Schools—Fiction. 2. Dinosaurs—Fiction.] I. Alley, R.W. (Robert W.), ill. II. Title.
PZ7.P97325Mq 1991 [E]—dc20 90-35771 CIP AC ISBN 0-02-775452-9

When Mrs. Toggle's children arrived at school in the morning, they found their teacher talking on her telephone.

"All right, Mr. Stickler," they heard her say. "We'll handle this as best we can. But I wish we had more time to get ready!" She hung up the phone.

"Good morning, Mrs. Toggle," the children said in their best morning voices.

Mrs. Toggle sank down into her chair. Her eyes were as big around as doughnuts. Then she blurted out one word: "Dinosaur!"

The children gathered around Mrs. Toggle's desk.
"Mrs. Toggle," said Paul. "Why did you say 'dinosaur'?"
Mrs. Toggle shivered. "We're going to have a new
student," she said. "It's a dinosaur!"

"But dinosaurs don't go to school," said Joey.

"I heard it from the principal himself," said Mrs. Toggle. "Mr. Stickler is never wrong."

"That's right," agreed Nina. "And he doesn't joke, either."

Caroline asked, "When is the dinosaur coming?"

"Today!" said Mrs. Toggle. "Oh, I knew things were too good to be true. Such a nice class, and just the right size. Now, this!"

The custodian, Mr. Abel, poked his head in the classroom door. "Excuse me, Mrs. Toggle," he said. "Mr. Stickler asked me to bring a desk for your new student."

The children and Mrs. Toggle went to the door to look.

Mrs. Toggle shook her head. "I'm not sure this desk will do."

"It isn't big enough," said Joey.

"Didn't Mr. Stickler tell you?" asked Nina.

"The new student is a dinosaur!" explained Paul.

"I see," said Mr. Abel. "A dinosaur will need a special desk. I'll get busy building one!"

"Thank you, Mr. Abel," said Mrs. Toggle. "Now I wonder what else we should do to get ready?"

"Why don't you go to the library?" suggested Mr. Abel. "You could read all about dinosaurs. Looking things up in books always helps me."

So Mrs. Toggle and her children hurried to the library. Mr. Paige, the librarian, greeted them. "Mrs. Toggle!" he said. "It's not your library day, is it?"

"You are quite right, Mr. Paige," said Mrs. Toggle. "But we have an emergency." She told Mr. Paige all about her new student, the dinosaur.

"That's wonderful!" said Mr. Paige. "There's nothing like a real event to encourage learning." He showed Mrs. Toggle and the children the shelf of dinosaur books. "You can find everything you need to know right here."

Mrs. Toggle looked doubtful. "Is there a book about how to teach a dinosaur?" she asked.

"You might have to write that one," admitted Mr. Paige.

Mrs. Toggle and the children settled down at a table with their dinosaur books.

"Dinosaurs died out sixty-five million years ago," Caroline read out loud.

Mrs. Toggle nodded. "Except this one, apparently."

Caroline added, "Some dinosaurs liked to live in groups with other dinosaurs."

Nina spoke up. "Then our dinosaur might be lonely. We should be nice to it and not choose it last for dodgeball teams."

"Yes," agreed Paul. "It will be the only reptile in our class. Being different can be difficult."

"Hey!" said Joey. "Snakes are reptiles! We could get a snake for our room to keep the dinosaur company."

Mrs. Toggle's face grew pale, and her eyes started to get big again.

"Or a turtle," suggested Nina quickly. "I don't think Mrs. Toggle wants a snake."

"Oh, sure," said Joey, patting Mrs. Toggle's arm. "We could get a turtle instead."

Mrs. Toggle smiled faintly.

Caroline said, "The word *dinosaur* means 'terrible lizard.'"

Mrs. Toggle groaned. "Not *too* terrible, I hope," she said. "Some dinosaurs were fierce, but some were peaceful and quiet. Perhaps our dinosaur will be the peaceful kind. Come, children, we had better return to our room to get ready. Thank you for your help, Mr. Paige."

"You're welcome," said Mr. Paige. "You might stop by the cafeteria and warn Mrs. Burns. If it's a big dinosaur, it probably eats a lot."

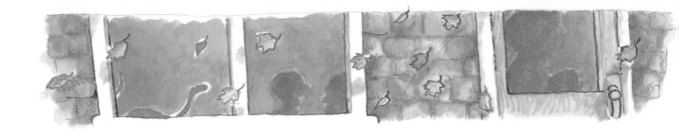

So Mrs. Toggle and the children trooped into the school kitchen. They found the cook, Mrs. Burns, tossing pizza dough.

"Mrs. Burns," said Mrs. Toggle, "have you heard about the new student?"

"Of course," replied Mrs. Burns. "Every year we have new students!"

"But this one is a dinosaur," said Mrs. Toggle.

"We thought you'd want to know," explained Joey, "because it might eat a lot."

"A dinosaur!" Mrs. Burns laughed. "That's a good one, Mrs. Toggle! But I won't worry about it until I find out if this dinosaur is a meat-eater or a vegetarian."

The children and Mrs. Toggle left Mrs. Burns, who was laughing hard and putting pepperoni on pizzas. "I wish I could laugh about my problems the way Mrs. Burns does," Mrs. Toggle told the children.

Back at their room, Mrs. Toggle and the children found Mr. Stickler waiting for them.

"Mrs. Toggle," said Mr. Stickler, "your new student has arrived."

"Mr. Stickler," said Mrs. Toggle, "I know I will learn to love my new student, as I love all my students. Still, I'm worried. Are you sure there is enough room in our school for this dino—"

"Mrs. Toggle," Mr. Stickler interrupted. "I'm surprised at you. Of course we make room in our school for any student who moves here. That's the rule!"

Mrs. Toggle sighed. "Oh, all right. Where *is* my new student?"

"Right here," said Mr. Stickler.
A little girl peeked out from behind him.
"But…," gasped Mrs. Toggle. "This…this is no…dino…saur!"

"Of course this is Dina Sawyer!" replied Mr. Stickler. "A little shy, but she'll get over it. Dina says she's afraid her new teacher won't like her!"

Mrs. Toggle's eyes widened with delight. "Dina Sawyer? Did you say 'Dina Sawyer'? Oh, my goodness! What a lovely, lovely name! I thought...! Not like her! Of course I like her! We all like Dina very much indeed, don't we, children?"

Mrs. Toggle smiled broadly at her new student. She turned to Mr. Stickler. "Thank you! Thank you so much! I couldn't be more pleased!"

Mr. Stickler returned to his office. Mrs. Toggle and the children showed the new student around the room.

"Dina," said Mrs. Toggle, "before we begin our lessons, I will tell you one thing I insist on. If I say something that doesn't make sense, ask questions. If you don't understand me the first time, ask me to repeat."

"Yes, Mrs. Toggle," said Dina.

Joey raised his hand. "Mrs. Toggle, where is the dinosaur?"

"There isn't one," said Mrs. Toggle. "I was mistaken."

"Too bad," said Joey. "Can we still get a turtle?"